TO FIND

THE ONE

by

R. A. Yates

This is dedicated to my wife and family. They inspire me every day to enjoy life.

I want to acknowledge the following: Dr Kelley for helping with medical information, Mrs. Lightsey for English and writing advice, and the following readers Elgin, Becky, Angel, Sasha, and Kaitlin. They encouraged me to finish this novel.

In a crowded school auditorium, the sporadic sound of clapping, echoes. Anthony "Tony" Meyers watched his son graduate high school. When his name was called, he stood and clapped his hands in pride to show his support for Zac.

Tony wished his wife, Sara, could have seen Zac graduate. When she died of cancer, a piece of Zac and Tony died with her. Zac was a first-year student when she passed away. It was hard to move on.

Tony worked longer hours at the construction company, to keep his mind busy. The demands of the company kept the family from traveling since the inception of the business.

When Sara was alive, she always wanted to go on vacation to the beach. Tony did not like vacationing or the beach but moved the company to Oceanside for Sara to live there. He built a house on the beach for her. That is where they raised Zac.

Tony's work ethic turned the company into a multimillion-dollar business. He wanted Zac to run the business when he retired.

Zac told his father, "I do not want the company. I have spent enough time working in it. There is something else for me in the world."

Zac's mom, Sara, wanted him to follow his dreams and be whatever he wanted. When she died, Zac no longer had her encouragement to push him.

After her death, Tony became depressed. He made some bad company decisions regarding projects. One of the contractors he worked with, advised him to leave the country. Tony needed a change of scenery to clear his mind.

"Your vice president can run things. Chad Layton will run the business for a brief period, it will be okay."

Traveling abroad was new to him. Tony's coffee farm was bought without seeing it, in 1994. It was nestled on the edge of a dormant volcano. When Tony saw the hillsides covered with tropical fauna, at the foot of a mountain, he thought he had reached paradise. He felt like he needed to buy it.

It was here that he met Maria, his second wife. She was less than five feet tall, dark hair, and very tan. Her kindness and caring won Tony's heart. After he had fallen while climbing to see coffee beans on the hillside, Maria took care of his wounds and nursed him back to health. It took him several days to recover from the fall.

Zac loved Maria. He missed his Sara, but Maria cared for him, like a mother. She was an excellent substitute for Sara.

At graduation, when Tony stood and whistled at the announcement of Zac's name, Maria sat and clapped for him. Zac could see her tears, as she sat on the front row.

Maria told Zac several times leading up to this night, "I did not finish school in my country. I want you to be educated. Then find a job that you enjoy doing."

After Tony confronted Zac with the offer to run the family business, Zac told his father, "I will make my own destiny. If needed, I will pay for my own education. That is how much it means to me."

Despite his father's pressure, he did as he promised. The next week, he packed his bags and drove hours to the reach the university.

At first, Tony thought he would return. He did, but only for holidays, to prove his independence. After the first year, Tony began paying Zac's tuition and the costs of classes. For that, Zac called his father more often and helped during the busy summer months.

As a science education major, he made the dean's list. His goal was to teach school. Most education classes had more girls than guys, on the roster. Presented with opportunities to meet so many new girls, he began dating more often.

Six feet tall, curly dark hair, and brown eyes, seemed to attract the attention of girls. He dated but never got serious. There were several who spent weekends with him. One, he brought home. She spent the weekend at the beach house and met Tony and Maria.

After two years in college, he began coming home every summer to help his father run the company. This was only in gratitude, for his father covering the costs of school.

Tony enjoyed the time he got with Zac but still hoped that he would change his mind about the business. During the time Zac did this, Tony stopped asking him. He knew the answer would be no. Tony said nothing about it, to keep him at home during the summer.

Zac earned his bachelor's degree in science education. Because he was anxious to begin working, he did not participate in the graduation ceremony. He chose to pick his diploma up from the registrar's office.

He graduated in December and received a job offer during the Christmas holiday. The school lost a teacher to an unexpected illness. That teacher retired early, and the school, Central High, needed a replacement.

Central HS is near Florala, a town sitting on the state line between Florida and Alabama. One of those towns named by location, like Texarkana.

The job location was ideal because Tony had a lake house there. The vacation home, sat on a lake. Tony called it the Lake House. He also has the Beach House and the Bay House, where he lives with Maria.

The first year passed quickly. The school had a younger faculty than he expected. Between the teen girls and the female faculty, he gathered a lot of attention the first year. He did date a couple of the teachers before learning, *do not date coworkers*.

As he settled into his job and learned a routine, he developed a quiet life of teaching during the week and staying at the lake house, alone.

Many evenings, he sat in a chair near the large windows, looking out at the lake. He watched the sunsets, drinking a glass of wine or beer.

Summers and holidays were spent in Oceanside with Tony, working in the construction company offices. Zac stayed at the beach house alone, eating with his dad and Maria, in the evenings.

He did not date often, only finding female companionship when needed. The number of girls having spent the night at the house, began to grow. Rumors began to spread that Zac was a womanizer.

Five years passed. He realized one day, when turning 30, that maybe he should settle into a relationship. He could get a roommate. Loneliness began to have an impact on his life.

During the summer, while he was in Oceanside, his phone rang. The principal, Mr. Lambert, was called.

"Zac, you have a big house by yourself. I need somewhere for the new middle school teacher to stay. There are no apartments available in town."

He agreed to allow the new teacher to stay at the lake house. There were four bedrooms in the house, plenty of room for someone else, for a little while at least. It would be nice to have someone to watch football and drink beer with.

The principal failed to inform him; it was girl. He did tell Zac to clean his act up.

"Someone in the community called me about the women leaving your house, in the early mornings. They are concerned about a womanizer teaching their daughter."

Zac promised to be more discreet and the principal promised to do damage control for him, in exchange for housing the new teacher.

When he returned to the lake, he called the principal and told him, "I am back in town. Give the new teacher, my address."

The next day, while he was drinking his morning coffee, there was a knock at the door. Wearing pajama pants, no shoes, and no shirt, he answered the door.

Standing outside the door was a five-foot-tall blonde. Looking like a cheerleader, she wore a pony tail, denim shorts, and a cut off t shirt. She smiled and introduced herself.

"I am Piper. You must be Zac. Mr. Lambert said I could stay here until I found an apartment."

Zac waved her in and walked her
to the other side of the lake house.
Carrying her suitcase, she walked with
him to her bedroom.

He gave her a tour of the house. He
showed her where to find anything she
needed. She would have her own
bathroom.

The tour was brief. All the while,
he did enjoy the way her ponytail bobbed
up and down, as she walked throughout
his home.

"Did you play sports in college?"
Zac thought she was very athletic.

She tells him she was a cheerleader and competed in gymnastics. She offers to share the cost of groceries, since there was going to be no cost for rent. He gave her a key and told her where to park her car.

She talked about her boyfriend back home. He could hear her on the phone at night, talking to him. When school started in the fall, the calls began to happen less often.

Piper planned to spend Thanksgiving with boyfriend. Zac was going to spend this holiday alone at the house, since she would be gone.

Unexpectedly, she returned on Thanksgiving. It was the evening. He had made roasted chicken, vegetables, and homemade bread.

When Piper came in, she was upset. She walked past him and went directly to her bedroom. He heard her crying from the kitchen. She looked like she had been crying when she came in.

Walking down the hall, he checks on her. She is crying, as she sits on her bed. He sits beside her and tries to comfort her.

"Come to the kitchen. It is Thanksgiving. Come have a glass of wine and tell me what's wrong."

Zac gets two wine glasses from the cabinet and pulls wine from the refrigerator. As he pours glasses half full, Piper comes to the kitchen. He hands her tissue and pats her on the shoulder.

When she pours herself a second glass, the story comes out. The surprise idea backfired. Her boyfriend had a girl at his house.

"I was going to surprise him. I walked in on him having sex, with another girl. I walked out, slamming the door behind me."

By this time, Zac began eating before the food got cold. Piper pulled a chair up beside him, as she drank her third glass of wine. She started eating off his plate. She was talking freely, now.

More wine and more food, led to them watching the sun set and the full moon appear, over the lake. She put her head on his shoulder.

He too, had drank too much wine. It influenced him to kiss her. There was no resistance in him to a pretty girl sharing her feelings, with him.

The light of the full moon reflected off their naked bodies, as they made love beneath the living room window. The last memory he has from thanksgiving night, is one of Piper moving back and forth, atop him, arching her back and moaning softly.

She slept with him every night after that and moved to his side of the house. They share a bedroom now since they are lovers.

She teaches in a different part of the school. So, they do not get to see each other on a typical school day. When the last bell rings, they see each other. This is the life they share together.

Five years pass quickly. During summers, they vacation together but do not visit each other's family. Piper asked Zac to take her to Oceanside. He avoids the topic. As another summer approaches, Zac is required to attend a teacher conference in New Orleans. She has made plans to go to the beach with some teacher friends.

It is the last day of school before summer break. His room is clean and ready for fall classes. Zac Myers, science teacher at Central, has the summer off after he attends a required workshop in New Orleans.

Zac pulls out of the faculty parking lot after loading his car and drives to the house he shares with his girlfriend of five years, Piper Davis. His phone rings as he pulls into the driveway. Hello, he recognizes the accent of his stepmother, Maria, who is from Costa Rica.

"Hey Zac, you need to listen closely. Your dad is sick. Please come home and run the company. He is dying." He can hear her sniffling as she talks to him. He tells himself, "My dad probably put her up to this."

They talk only briefly as he tells her, "I am not interested in running the company, Maria. Let Chad run it. I need to go inside and pack for my workshop. We can talk another time. In fact, when I get back from New Orleans, I will see dad." He knew it was serious based on the emotion in Maria's voice.

Several years earlier, after graduating high school, he and his father had an argument over the company. The argument was fueled by Tony trying to force the company on Zac.

The confrontation between Zac and his father, led to him going to college to become a teacher. Zac left home and returned during the summers and Christmas.

Since then, Zac and his father Tony, have had a very splintered relationship. It is difficult for them to talk any length of time without one of them becoming mad.

Following the death of Zac's mother, Tony became lonely and unhappy. It was the loneliness that made Maria an asset to him and to Zac. She was a peacemaker by nature. She is the voice of reason and encourages them to talk and maintain their relationship.

In 1985 Tony started the company and worked it into a multi-million-dollar business. He wanted to be a father son ran company. Zac wanted no part of it.

It is the company that prevented the family from vacationing over the years. He did not want the long days and extended time required to get properties, bid on contracts, and negotiate with customers. He chose the profession that would allow him to be free during the summers.

Five years ago, as a favor, he housed a new elementary teacher in his family's lake house. Piper was several years his junior. She was young, blonde, and tan. Her complexion was brown from the years spent as a lifeguard on the beaches near Tampa.

In the beginning, they shared the four-bedroom house and the food. However, after too many glasses of wine one evening, they ended up in bed together. That was the beginning.

The house was built when Zac was in elementary school. It sits on the largest natural lake in the state. Half of the lake is in Alabama and half of it is in Florida.

His girlfriend Piper loves the large windows, with view of the lake. They have made love many times beneath them, watching the setting sun.

Grabbing his bag, he walks up the stairs of the lake house. When he reaches the double doors decorated with seashells, Piper runs past. She is topless, wearing only the bottom of a yellow bikini. He drops his bag and hurries through the door.

Chasing her down the hallway and into the master bedroom, they fall together onto the bed. After rolling over onto her, he says, "I love you."

With her beneath him, he gazes into her blue eyes. Piper applies a gentle tug and removes her suit. Moments later, their naked bodies are now moving in unison. The gentle rhythm of their skin moving against each other, fills the bedroom.

Afterwards, they do not talk much. She rolls over as he is falling asleep, and whispers to him, "I love you; I want us to get married and have a family together." Zac hears her but does not respond.

The next morning the sound of the shower running and the smell of coffee, wakes him up.

Now sitting up in bed, he sees her stepping out of the shower. He invites her

to go with him to New Orleans for the
teacher conference. Watching, as towels
off from the shower, "hey, how about a
quick one before I have to leave town?"
She looks at him, "I do not have time to
play with you.

Zac tells her, "I have a
workshop in New Orleans this weekend.
You could go with me. "Piper responds, "I
have a beach trip plan with some of the
teachers on the other hall."

Zac nods and tells her that is okay.
He then tells her about the phone call he
got from his stepmom Maria. "She called
on the way home. Dad is sick. When I get

back from New Orleans, I am going home and seeing everyone."

Piper tells him, "I love you why don't you marry me? Take me to meet your parents." Zac is surprised by her proposal to get married. "I love you Piper, but I do not think I am ready to marry anyone right now. Aren't you happy?"

The excitement in Piper's face fades following his response to the proposal. She glances at him then walks out of the room and slams the door. Zac shrugs and goes into the kitchen to get a cup of coffee.

He can hear Piper in the other room as she talks to herself and packs her beach bag for the trip with her friends. Moments later the door opens and Piper walks through the kitchen wearing her yellow bikini.

She stops next to the kitchen table where Zac is drinking coffee and tells him, "When you return, we will talk about this again. I am ready to be a wife and a mom. This is not over. If you do not feel what I feel, when we are together, we may need to part."

He knew he had made a mistake, but he also did not have time to take care of that problem right now he would have to wait. She returned to the kitchen after packing her bag. She told him goodbye as she left the house slamming the door and calling him a jackass.

Looking at his watch, he jumps up, hurries around the house grabbing the things he needed for his conference and dashes out the door.

Late, he is now having to make up last time and get to the Crescent city for the beginning of the conference.

Two hours into the trip, Zac's phone rings. He places it on speaker. Hey Chad, how are things going? What is going on with dad because Maria sounded upset when she called me earlier.

Chad tells him about his father becoming weak and collapsing in his office. Your dad was telling me what his plans were, when he gripped his shoulder and failed to the floor. By the time Chad finished the story, Zac was even more concerned about his dad. Chad finished their conversation by telling him the company is stronger than ever.

Zac, you need to call Maria or see him awhile. He needs rest period I can run veins until he gets strong enough to come back.

Chad Layton has never been someone that Zac liked. He has a cutthroat methodology of doing business. He has beady eyes, pale skin, and the high voice. Any conversation with him was suspect because Zac had heard about some of the manipulation of contracts done behind his father's back.

It is not his name on the company. It is the Myers family name attached to the company and all the business that the company does. Once Chad dismissed the secretary caught him making side deals at work on the company's time. You see, Chad owned his own construction company. Some of the company's employees said he was secretly sabotaging projects and buying some of the overage of lumber, for his own company.

Now, Zac knew he needed to go home after the trip. Chad could be stealing from the company if his dad is sick.

The phone call between Zac and Chad ended abruptly because the phone signal had dropped. Picking up his phone, he saw several texts from Piper with apologies hearts and kisses. There were several attachments of engagement rings and other types of wedding rings. When he saw this, he turned away and placed his phone face down.

Following the dismissal of the secretary, he reached out to speak to her. Susan Madrid had been with the company for many years and was a faithful employee.

"Susan, can you tell me about that day? I do not believe you should have been fired."

He could hear her struggling to tell the story. She was sobbing. Zac called the human resources department personally for her to get severance.

She used to keep soft drinks and candy in her desk just for him. When he was younger and he came to the office,

Susan was always kind to him and would take up time talking and entertaining him, while his father was in meetings. He had many fond memories of her in the office.

She began telling him about the events of that day. "The office door was open. I heard Mr. Layton on the phone. He said, the old man does not know I am sending material to my warehouse. With any luck, my company can make a million this year."

She then asked Chad if she needed to put together a purchase agreement and contact dispatch for a shipment. He became furious and slammed the cell phone down. This caused it to slide across the carpeted floor. When it came to rest at her feet, the screen said Layton construction.

"He fired me when I read the screen aloud. I was doing my job." She began to cry. Zac reassured her that it would be all right.

For the last two years, she has been the school secretary. He had made some phone calls to get her a job at his school.

Zac had not noticed that the sun was setting. Ahead a sign read New Orleans city limits. This time away from Piper might be good for their relationship he tells himself

Ahead of him was the exit sign, *French Quarter Vieux Carre.*

The GPS in his car took him down Conte Street. Halfway down that road, he had to stop for a man kneeling in the road and throwing up. There are bars all along the street. The music fills the air and the car.

Looking up at the street sign, it read Bourbon Street. He always enjoyed the sights and sounds of the world-famous attraction.

Tapping on his window causes him to turn his head. A police officer is signaling for him to move on down the road. A group of girls jumped in front of his car, Woo, they lifted their shirts exposing their breasts before giving him a peace sign.

At the end of the street, stands a gold statue of someone riding a horse. The smell of food and sound of jazz fill his car. The GPS chimes, declaring Decatur Street, turn right. Destination on the right.

The sights and sounds of New Orleans, change after sunset. The music gets louder, the drinks flow faster, and the food is more decadent. The atmosphere is one that encourages people to overindulge in many things, mostly alcohol and food. It is a city for those who are fat and sassy.

The carousel bar on the ground floor is a historic part of the hotel. As he drove under the front awning, near the valet, he looked up the steps into the foyer. He could see a large chandelier hanging from the ceiling.

Someone opened his car door. "Sir, I will park your car and have your luggage unloaded. Here is your parking receipt."

The valet took his keys, while someone carried his luggage into the lobby, near the front desk, to check in.

The sound of gunfire caused him to turn his head. It was a truck that had just pulled into the parking lot and backfired. The truck behind him was the source. The female driver screamed in surprise. Zac smiles at her as she steps out of the truck. She returns the friendly gesture.

After walking up the stairs into the lobby and checked in with the front desk. With his key, he is escorted by a bellhop to the nearest elevator. The bellhop looks at him and says, "follow me Sir and I will take you to your room."

As they were waiting for the elevator, the woman from the truck is now inside the elevator with him. Another bellhop stood next to her. Once the elevator door opened, they all four entered the elevator. The number three was lit.

Once they had reached the third floor the door is open to the hallway leading to all the rooms. Zac motions for the bellhop and the woman to step out of the elevator, first.

All of them walked down the hallway to find their rooms. The bellhop turned to the woman and said, "Ma'am this is your room number 315."

Zac continued walking with the second bellhop until they had reached his room, 318.

He gives the bellhop a tip and entered his room. After closing the door, he puts his luggage on the bed and sits down. The day had already been eventful. Sitting on the bed, his phone rang.

"Hello Piper, what is going on? I thought you were mad with me."

As he sat on the bed listening to her through the speaker, he starts to look at the text messages she had sent him earlier. All the pictures were of diamond rings engagement rings or wedding rings. He closed his all the messages and glances out the window while she talks to him.

Piper tells him, "I found the most gorgeous rings at the jewelry store near the beach. Forget about earlier I love you." He is gazing out the window now. Piper says, "I said do you still want me to come to New Orleans?" Zac, not paying attention, says, "yeah whatever." The pause following his response gives him a moment to think about what he said. "Wait, hold it, do not come. I am remarkably busy. I do not have time to see you."

It is too late. She hung up.

He tries to message her after the phone call but gets no response.

After waiting briefly for a response from Piper, he opens his suitcase and unpacks for the workshop. He realizes that it is suppertime as his stomach begins to growl. He decides to freshen up in the bathroom, change his shirt, and leave his room for dinner.

After locking his door, he walks down the hall, and catches the elevator to the lobby to find the nearest restaurant.

Waiting at the elevator is the woman who had shared the elevator with him. Both stare at the lights above the elevator door indicating the elevator's location.

He looks at the woman wearing a summer dress, make up, and heels. Like many leaving the hotel, she looks like she was going out for the evening. He asked if she was going to the Cafe down the street. She looked back at him and said, "Yes."

"It is easy to get there from here," Zac introduced himself to the woman. Smiling, he says, "I am Zac. It is nice to meet someone on their first trip to the Crescent City."

She extends her hand, "Kimberley, it is nice to meet you, as well."

When they reached the lobby Zac tells her, "Since it is dinner, and this is your first time in town, why don't you let me show you where it is? I will buy you supper." They exited the hotel and walked to the cafe. She told him that the trip took longer than she had planned and that she taught at a small county school in South Carolina.

During their walk to the restaurant, he gives her a brief history of the city. He tells her about the French and Spanish influence and how many of the chefs call New Orleans home. Before reaching the café, Zac tells her something the first-time visitors should know.

"I do hope this spicy food is not a problem for you. New Orleans cuisine is wonderful but can be too much for some."

Once inside the door of the restaurant the chatter of conversation, the sound of glasses clinking, and the smell of foods being served, fills her senses.

The restaurant had brick cobbled walls, dark wood floors, and tables lit by hanging Tiffany lights. Kimberly scanned the room and soaked up the atmosphere before they were seated.

"Come on, they have our table ready. I called ahead." The host greeted them and walked them to their table. She introduced their server.

"This is David, he will be your server tonight. I hope you enjoy your meal."

The table covered with a white cloth had two glasses turned upside down on it. Water and silverware wrapped by a napkin were also set on the table. The server asked them if he could start them with drinks and if they were interested in an appetizer.

"Give us a few minutes to look at the menu and then come back please, he told him." At that, the server left to address another table of customers.

Kimberley looked at him, "I do not know what to order. What would be a good dish to try?" She looked at the tables near them and their food.

He asks her, "how about rice? Do you like rice? If you do, red beans and rice is an excellent choice. I will ask them to give you mild not spicy." She looks at him and agrees.

Zac tells the server when he returns. Kimberly scans the room and admires the architecture. He glances at her. For the past five years, there has been only Piper.

His phone alerts him of a message. Pulling the phone from his pants, the screen displays, *I miss you. Call me, Piper.* Zac responds to this by turning his phone off.

David, the server, places the bowl of red beans on the table in front of her. She looks down, smells it, then smiles at him.

He notices her grey eyes and the highlights of Auburn in her brown hair. He smiles back at her, "I hope you like it."

Later, Zac orders Key Lime Pie for dessert. They share funny stories of teaching and the challenges of being a teacher. She tells him that she lives less than an hour from Myrtle Beach.

When the check comes for dinner, they both reached for it. Her hand ends up on top of his. She withdraws it and looks at him. He notices that she has blushed. "Sorry." Suddenly there is a tense awkwardness.

Kimberly asked him if he is ready to walk back to the hotel. It is late and we have meetings tomorrow. He nods back at her, pays the bill, and they walk back. They talk only briefly on the return trip.

"Thank you for showing me the restaurant. The soup was good, still a little spicy. Would you let me buy you dinner before going home?" Zac tells her not to worry about it.

After reaching the hotel and taking the elevator to their floor, Zac speaks to her after exiting the lift. We will bump into each other at the conference. She smiles and turns and walks to her room saying, "Maybe."

A sense of guilt fills him after he closes the door to his room. There was a certain attraction that he felt to Kimberly. Piper is his girlfriend, though.

Pulling his phone out, he notices the missed call and text messages from Piper. He thinks to himself, "what have I done wrong. It was just dinner. We did not have sex."

It had been a nice evening. He did not read all the messages from Piper. He tells himself; they are all the same. I love you; I forgive you, or I still want to marry you. Instead of reading all the messages, he showers and goes to bed.

Tomorrow, meetings throughout the day. At 11:00 PM, he finally gets in bed, turns the lamp off, and closes his eyes.

The next morning, he leaves the hotel and walks to the Convention Center. On the way, he calls home to talk to his stepmom, and check on his father.

"How is dad, Maria? I wanted to see if he has improved." She tells him that Tony has virtual meetings scheduled for the afternoon.

"Your dad would trust Chad, but it is hard after he fired Susan."

In the background, Zac can hear his father yelling at the home health nurse. "Get off me, I do not need you to do that. Maria, is that Zac? Tell him to come home and help me." Tony's voice began to trail

off as Maria walked through the house.
She told him that his father was improving
and seemed to get stronger each day.

Zac asks her, "what exactly
happened to him?" Maria tells him that it
was a heart attack and that sometime soon,
will need surgery for a blocked artery.

By the time the call ends, Zac
reaches the Convention Center. There, he
spent the entire day in meetings. Just
before the end of the first day session, Zac
sees Kimberly in the Convention Center
leaving a side exit. Walking back to the
hotel, he looks for her along the way
hoping to see her.

He does not. When he returns to the hotel, he showers and puts on slacks but no shirt. His phone rings. It is Piper. He answers.

"Hello piper, how was the beach? Oh, I saw the pictures of rings. We really need to talk." She was telling him about the beach jewelry store and wedding venues when there was a knock at his door.

Opening it, he finds Kimberley. She is wearing an emerald, green summer dress and heels.

Meanwhile, he still has Piper on the phone. She is going on about chiffon, lace, and wedding bands. She is giving details that Zac is unable to even understand.

For some reason, in the middle of the yes, sure, sounds nice, rapid fire, he stops her. "Listen, I need to go. Someone is at the door." He lies rather than tell the truth.

"Are you going to ask me in?" she speaks.

He smiles and motions for her to enter. She looks at him and says "do you have plans tonight? I would like to buy you dinner, so you can tell me more about New Orleans."

"Okay, I would love to show you around."

She smiles at him after he agrees. Zac feels a little nervous, standing in a hotel room shirtless, with a strange woman. He has not felt anything like this since the day he met Piper. He slips on a shirt, and they leave the hotel.

While they were walking down Decatur Street, she tells him about the small town she grew up in and the high school where she works. He asks her how small Dillon is, because he is from a small town in Florida that has two red lights.

He asks her, "do you have any family there?"

She looks away and changes the subject. "What is the importance of that cannon up there? Is it to protect the church across the street?"

Zac tells her about Jackson Square, Napoleon, and how the city has changed hands over the many years it has existed.

While he is telling her about the church, a man walks up to them and tells them to move outside the gate. They are locking up for the evening.

"I smell coffee. Where is it coming from?" she says.

Zac smiles and tells her, "It is Cafe du Monde. They are known for coffee and beignets. Come on."

With that said, they walk to the coffee stand passing a man playing a jazz standard on his saxophone. Zac could not name the song, but he recognized it. Dropping $5 into the man's hat, he tells him, "You sound good." He nods in appreciation and continues to play.

Once inside, she asks him about the powder sugar coating the floor. As they walked to an open table, they pass a group of people eating beignets. He hears Kimberley say, "Now I know where it is coming from."

Zac orders two coffees and a saucer of beignets. The waiter returns with a tray carrying water, coffee, and the sugary treats. Kimberley was apprehensive at first, but soon had eaten them all. Zac looks at her with sugar on her nose and cheek, eating.

He picks up a napkin, dipping the tip in his water, and gently cleans her nose and cheek. Telling her, "It is good. I know."

She blushes, laughs for a moment, and turns away before saying, "I do not always eat like this. I do have manners."

After the appetizer at the café, they walk to the restaurant. "Follow me. It is just up the street, on the second floor over an antique shop."

During dinner, Zac drank two glasses of wine while Kimberly drank several whiskey sours. It was getting late, and Kimberley had drunk enough, in his opinion. She was enjoying her first trip to the French Quarter. She is not the first or last to overdo it, here.

It was at this time that he decided it was time for them to go back to the hotel. He did not want her to be hungover at the morning meetings.

He paid the bill, escorted Kimberly down the stairs, and out onto the street for the walk back. She began to weave as she walked. To steady herself, she grabbed his arm. It took a little while longer to make it back to the hotel, but they made it.

Luckily, the lobby was empty. Taking her around the waist, he walked her to her room. "Where is your key? I need to get you into your room." He looks through her handbag for a few moments. She has now sat down and is leaning against the door to her room.

He looks down at her, "Come on. I cannot find your key. You will have to sleep

this off in my room. I will sleep in the chair."

After getting her up from the floor, they walk the short distance to his room. He holds the door open for her to enter. She walks into the room, pulling her shoes off.

Standing in the bathroom she tells him, "I am going to shower if that is all right with you." Zac tells her sure and sits on the foot of the bed to relax.

It had been a long day of lectures by teachers about topics mundane and mind numbing. He fell asleep during one of the afternoon sessions. He laid back on the bed and closed his eyes. The droning sound of the shower running in the bathroom, put him to sleep.

When the shower stopped, he woke. Opening his eyes, he sees Kimberly is holding his hand. She looks down at him, "Is it still ok for me to stay here tonight? I still cannot find my key and it is late."

He lets go of her hand and sits up. She is standing next to the bed, wearing only a towel. She smiles at him and releases the towel, allowing it to fall to the floor.

He pulls her near him, cupping her hips in his hands. Pulling her down on top of him, with his arms wrapped around her, he rolls her over. He begins to kiss her breasts, then her neck, before kissing her deeply on the mouth.

On top of her now, he is looking into those steel grey eyes. The same eyes he admired from across the dinner table, earlier. He noticed then, how candlelight flickered in her eyes. They were mesmerizing that evening.

"I learn more about you every time we are together. I wish this week would last longer. Kimberly, you are something else."

Moments later, Zac has removed the remainder of his clothes and Kimberly has climbed atop him, straddling his hips, moving like she is on a slow galloping horse. She moans louder as her movements become more aggressive. The pace grows to an apex, ending in a final thrust.

She collapses on him, pressing her face against him as their heaving chests move against each other, trying to recover. Their bodies glistening with sweat, they fall asleep in an embrace. The climax of this workday was in each other's arms.

He wakes the next morning before her. It had been years since he had slept with anyone other than Piper. Looking at her nude body next him in the bed, he notices the wrinkles and stretch marks. An indication that she was not young like Piper. Her perfume reminded him of spring flowers, gardenias. His mom loved gardenias and had several shrubs planted in his family's yard.

The phone in the room rang, waking them both. Kimberley jumped up and began to dress.

"Hello, this is Mr. Meyers." He quickly slammed the phone down at the same moment someone knocked at the door.

Before he could put clothes on, the door opened.

It was Piper. "Surprise! I came to see…what is going on?" Piper shouted several expletives, said something about trust and stormed out of the room.

Kimberley watched Piper leave. She said nothing. Walking into the bathroom, she returned with her handbag and pulled out a wedding ring. Zac was speechless. He did not know what to say.

She looked at him after walking to the door. "Do not try to find me. Yes, I am married. I had a wonderful time with you

Zac. Another time in my life, we could have been more. Goodbye."

All he could do is lay back and think about how his life changed suddenly. He reaches for his phone, hoping that Piper would talk to him. She sends him a text minutes later.

I told you that I was going to come to New Orleans to see you. I did not think you would cheat on me. I will have moved out by the time you get back. We are through.

He dresses and goes down the hall to see Kimberly. She is gone. The house cleaners are cleaning her room.

Kimberley never really unpacked her travel bag. When she left Zac, she simply grabbed her bag and walked to the elevator to check out. Reaching the lobby desk, she wrote a note and left it for him.

She drove to the interstate, thinking of Zac only one time. When she crossed the Alabama state line, the thought of Zac and walking down the cobblestone of Bourbon Street, holding his hand, came to mind. She smiles, to acknowledge that she was taken with him, if only for the weekend.

Ahead, there were miles of interstate to drive. New Orleans will remain a memory. No strings attached was the agreement she made with herself. Afterall, she has a husband, and they have an open relationship.

After watching Piper storm from his room and the discovery that Kimberly is married, Zac did not feel excited about the remaining time he had in the city.

He calls home to check on his dad. Maria answers the phone.

"Hello Maria, tell dad I am coming back early. In fact, I am going to spend some time with you and dad before I go back to work."

After gathering his luggage, he leaves the room and goes to the service desk.

The man behind the desk gives him an envelope and tells him that a woman left it for him to get at checkout. When Zac reaches his vehicle, he opens the letter.

Zac,

the last couple of days were wonderful. Thank you for showing me around the town and introducing me to the local cuisine. I am sorry about your girlfriend. You are a great guy, but I am married. It is time for me to leave before I hurt someone else. This was meant to be fun. Nothing serious. Please do not try to find me,

Kimberly

During the drive home, he thinks about Piper and Kimberly, reliving the horror of being caught in bed naked with another woman. The sense of guilt begins to fill his stomach. There was never a promise between them of matrimony, but the guilt still mounted.

At the same time, he is strongly attracted to Kimberly and did not know she was married. He had guilt for the damage he may have caused.

When he passed the Alabama State line and was driving through Mobile, he called his dad and Maria.

While in New Orleans, his stepmother Maria, sent him a message about his father, Tony.

Update on your dad, he hurt his shoulder when he collapsed. A therapist comes to the house for his physical therapy. Do not worry about your dad, he is a tough man. He will recover.

While Tony heals, Chad is running the company for the brief time. When he can return to his normal routine of meetings and running the company, the doctor will release him. Meanwhile, many of the real estate bids and major decisions, have been put on pause. Tony's heart does not need the stress of daily meetings and negotiations done within a normal day.

His shoulder will not allow him to do the job of managing the company, for now. So, Tony has been unhappy and unable to do what he loves, work.

When Zac is within an hour of his childhood home, he calls his parents.

"Hey dad, I am close to home. I am going to stay awhile and help, so you don't overdo it."

This gets Tony excited. He tells him how much it will help, to have someone he can trust to make big decisions for the company. Tony tells him that Chad made a mess of things while he was in the hospital.

When Zac reaches the Oceanside city limits sign, he tells his dad goodbye. He is near home now.

When Tony and Maria got married, Tony had a house built on the bay for them. Maria did not feel comfortable living with the memory of his first wife, in the beach house.

Zac spent most of his childhood in the beach house. It held memories of many happy days. It is also the house where his mom died. So, it is a solemn place as well.

When Tony tells Maria that Zac is coming to stay for a couple of weeks, she begins to flutter around the house preparing for his arrival. She places towels in the guest bathroom and plans Zac's favorite dishes for dinner.

Maria has always desired to be the mom that Zac no longer has. She does not want to replace his decease mom, just fill in the best way possible. He loves Maria because she has always fussed over him and encouraged him to be the best version of himself.

Meanwhile, Tony informs Chad that Zac is coming in to help negotiate the contract for the new condominium on the beach. Chad does not share the same enthusiasm for Zac's arrival. He tells Tony on the call, "I can oversee this deal. You do not have to get Zac involved." Tony tells him curtly, "yes I do."

The call to Chad ends, as Zac pulls into the driveway, after entering the code in the box. Pulling down the driveway, past palm trees and tropical shrubs, causes him to remember the times he

skateboarded the driveway every
weekend.

At the end, sits the large bay home
with a circle drive and fountain. Maria and
Tony walk out to welcome him when he
arrives.

"We are so happy that you have
come to stay awhile, Zac." Maria walks up
to him, wraps her arms around him, and
kisses him on the cheek.

Zac looks at his dad and tells him,
"Dad, I know we have had our moments,
but you have to take care of yourself."

It took several hours to drive from
New Orleans to Oceanside. Zac missed

lunch and the smell of shrimp from Maria's kitchen, made his hunger worse. When he tells Maria he can smell it, she tells him that she has made shrimp tacos, just for him.

"Stay with us Zac, do not go back to teach. I will make shrimp tacos for you, all the time."

All he can do is smile, wrap an arm around her, and kiss the top of her head. Maria was short by family standards. She was normal for someone from Costa Rica.

Maria led him to the kitchen after he brought his one piece of luggage inside. He gulped down five shrimp tacos, with vegetables and tortilla chips. After eating, he pulled a couple of drinks out the refrigerator and walked to his dad's office.

Tony was writing on a legal pad when Zac entered and sat in one of the leather chairs. His dad looked up.

"Look, help me run the company. You can live in the beach house across the street. It has always been your favorite. I cannot live there after your mom died from cancer in it."

Zac did not promise to stay beyond the summer, as they talked about the company's business. There were projects finishing, some still in construction, and more importantly, some that needed attention.

He offered to help until Tony could take it back. He found that Chad's way, made a mess of some things. Zac told his father he could fix it and give the accounts attention.

At the end of their talk, his dad asked him why he was suddenly interested in the family business. The only answer he could give was, "I do not want the company to be your end."

You have sacrificed everything to be successful." His dad asked why the sudden interest in the company? Are you still seeing Piper?

He chose not to share with him the story of how they had broken up. He answered him. "No dad, Piper and I are not together anymore. She moved out while I was in New Orleans."

Because of his shoulder injury from the collapse, Tony could not sign papers and conduct the transactions the way he normally does for the company. Three times a week, a physical therapist has performed in home therapy on him.

Tony gave Zac a detailed report on the active construction transactions. Zac looked through the report as they walked to his father's multimedia office.

"Zac, the new apartment complex on the beach was finished. All Chad had to do was get the signatures. He made a mess with the paperwork and with the clients."

That evening after the conversation in Tony's office, Zac, Maria, and Tony ate together. That was the first time is several years. He slept in his old bedroom, the one he claimed after the Bay house was built. The house was built right after Tony and Maria got married.

The next morning, he was woken by shouting. Zac rushed from his room, running through the house, hoping his dad had not collapsed again. As he came near, he found that the profanity and shouting was coming from his dad's office.

"Why are you being so rough?"

The sounds of him grunting and shouting in discomfort, led to Zac stepping into the room. Standing in the office doorway, he says, "hey, I came to check on you. Sounds like torture from the other side of the house."

The woman holding Tony's arm like a wrestling hold, looked up. She smiled warmly and said, "I am Mya, your dad's therapist. Your dad is acting a bit. I am not hurting him. You must be Zac; your dad has been talking about you."

When she looked back at Tony, she told him therapy is finished, for today. "Do your exercises and I will see you in a couple of days." She smiled at Zac, grabbed her bag with Oceanside Medical on the side, and walked toward the front door.

Before reaching the threshold of the atrium, she turns back to say, "nice to meet you Zac. Your dad did not say you were here."

Chad walked through the door when Mya opened it to leave. Zac picked up a pastry and a cup of coffee from a tray, near the door.

During the meeting, the three men met in Tony's office to discuss the current projects and their progression. When they had all been seated, Tony reached to grab a remote control. When he pressed the button, a screen lowered from the ceiling. A projector was turned on. He began to speak.

"The company's golf condominium project and real estate deals are on hold. We have not followed county code. This must be fixed." Tony told them how the company had not been up to his standard. The meeting was meant to let them both know what they were expected to do. Make it right.

Tony spoke again, "I asked Chad to come so that we could both tell you what we need over the next couple of weeks to months."

Zac listened to data about costs, materials, and processes for two hours. At the end of the meeting, when Tony left the room, Chad asked him about Piper. He asked him why he was not with her, at the Lake house.

Zac told him they were not together. He said, "we broke up Chad.

That is all there is to tell. I do not think we will be back together again."

Tony returned. "Chad, aren't you going to the office? I need you to check with one of the contractors and make some phone calls for me." Chad left and Zac went to his bedroom to pack his suitcase.

"Dad, I need to go back to the lake house and switch clothes if I am going to help you do business."

Maria came in while he was talking. "Leave your clothes here and I will wash them. Just get your office clothes to help your dad. Hurry back. We will miss you."

Maria walked with him out. Carrying his suitcase, he left the bay house. Driving up the cobblestone driveway, he entered the highway and started the journey back.

He felt like he needed to make a new beginning. The lake house held memories of Piper and the life they shared. How would he cope with the memories?

The drive along the beach is beautiful. Cars have filled the parking lots and the beach goers' line both sides of the road.

All of them are hoping to get a good spot on the white sand of Panama

City Beach. The sand, sun, and sound of the beach during the summer, is irreplaceable.

As he passes the city limits sign, his phone rings. It is Piper. "Hello."

The soft voice on the other end of the phone began, "Hello Zac, it has been a few days and I have waited to call you. Realize that you betrayed me and the relationship we had."

She told him there would be a time coming when she would get back at him. "Send anything of mine to my parents in Pensacola. I will message the address to you. Do you have anything to say for yourself before I hang up?"

There were many things he wanted to say but none of them would have been satisfactory to her. He wanted to say he still loved her. Instead, he said nothing other than, "I wish you to find someone to love you." That was the kindness he had for the memories of good times shared.

On the other end of the phone. All he heard was click. He glanced over and dropped his phone in the passenger seat. When he looked up, it was too late.

The dump truck in front of him had stopped. He could not move fast enough to engage his break. He collided with the truck, crushing the front of his car.

He remembers trying to slam on the brakes, The sound of metal crushing, and pain. There are memory flashes of Rescue squads and the sound of sirens.

Opening his eyes, he sees a woman in scrubs. She looks at him smiling, "hello, Mr. Myers, I am your nurse. I am here to give you medicine in your IV. You were in an accident."

He looks up at the ceiling and goes back to sleep. Someone is tapping him on his hand, and he opens his eyes again, Mr. Meyers, I am Doctor Kelley. You have fractured your patella, you know knee cap. We are keeping you overnight for observation."

The doctor tells him he will be off his feet for 4-6 weeks. He will need physical therapy and cannot drive for a while. He speaks to someone sitting at the foot of the bed. Tony and Maria have come to the hospital.

His dad walks over to the bed, "well son, you do not halfway do anything. Good news is not surgery."

Tony tells him that Maria has prepared his old bedroom for an extended stay, through summer.

Maria tells him, "Dr. Kelley says no driving for a while."

Tony and Maria seemed to enjoy fussing over him. Maria brings him his favorite snacks, books to read, and crosswords. Tony brings him the prospectus for the beach projects. After a couple of hours, a nurse comes in his room to tell him that physical therapy and a case nurse would be through soon.

The nighttime brought pain. His head hurt from the mild concussion and his leg now showed the signs of a patella fracture.

Good morning, Dr Kelly and breakfast seemed to arrive at the same time.

The doctor told him to stay off his leg, do the therapy, and return to his office in six weeks. "You are going to be okay, just follow up with me."

By lunch, he is discharged from the hospital. A nurse comes into his room pushing a wheelchair. She told him to put his clothes on, to leave.

Tony and Maria were waiting for him when he reached the lobby. They loaded him into the car and took him back to the house. On the way home, Tony drove by the garage where Zac's car was sitting.

"Zac, your car is totaled. We will get you another to replace it. After looking at it, I am glad you are all right."

Zac after seeing it says, "yeah, I'm glad to be her."

All that was salvaged from the accident, were valuables like his wallet, glasses, and phone. Tony gives Zac's phone to him, in the car. Zac begins reading any messages he may have missed while in the hospital. There is one from Piper.

I heard of the accident. Hoping you are all right. I am not insensitive to a true tragedy. Piper.

During the ride back to the Bay House, Zac thought about the message from Piper. He read it several times, deciphering any hidden messages in the text. The afternoon passed as slept, after returning home.

Moving around in the house on crutches, kept him from doing many things. Tony and Maria made sure he took his medicine. His stepmom enjoyed having someone to cook for since his father did not eat big meals. This gave Maria an opportunity to cook pasta dishes,

Fajitas, and states. Maria enjoyed cooking for him.

On Monday, Tony finished his therapy with Mya. He came to Zac's room to tell him. Zac sitting in the courtyard, near the pier, was drinking coffee and eating a pastry prepared by Maria.

"I have finished my physical therapy. Tomorrow, you will start your therapy. When I finished today, Mya told me before she left."

Maria called for Tony to come to the phone before Zac could talk to him about the session and what Mya said.

Back in his childhood home, memories came back, of the time following his mom's death. She died of cancer in the beach house. Her bedroom had a window looking out over the beach. She spent mornings and evenings watching the water. When her health was good, she talked about taking a cruise trip to an exotic island, staying in a tiny hut. She craved solitude and wanted to have Tony travel with her.

He would not leave the company to travel. She died of cancer and heartbreak from broken promises, made by her Zac's dad. Tony said they would visit every country in Europe. They did not.

Many evenings she would think of traveling, sit in her lounge chair on the back deck, and imagine a far-off island, as she looked across the water. She died at home unable to leave her bed.

Hospice allowed her to be at home with Tony and Zac, in her final days. Tony grieved. He put a black pillowcase on her pillow. He mourned for a year.

When Zac was a baby, Tony decided to invest in a coffee farm. The Costa Rican farm made money every year. The dividends helped Tony build his construction company and bid more than the competitors.

One year after Zac's mom, Sara's death, Tony decided to leave the beach house and company to see the coffee farm. Two days later, he is walking down a hillside, looking at green coffee beans.

Before making the trip, he contacted his representative in the country. Maria was the one who gave him the tour years ago.

Maria showed Tony the plantation, introduced him to the workers, and how to roast beans to sell at market. She offered to show him around the small town located near the plantation. That meeting led to more trips out of country.

Weekend trips led to their marriage and
life together.

When Zac asked his dad why,
Tony told him that his mom will be
forgotten or replaced.

He said, "your mom would not
want my life to end because of her
sickness. She would want me to enjoy my
life enough for the both of us."

Maya arrived the next day at the Bay House and started his physical therapy. Leg lifts, static quad exercises, and learning to move on crutches, absorbed the entire session. After she left, he felt good until the next morning when all the soreness arrived. She came back the next day to work out his soreness from the therapy.

Mya asked Zac, "are an only child? Your dad talked about you all the time when I came."

He replied, "yes, you are looking at the only child and heir to my dad's business. Whether I want it or not, he intends to give it to me. I want to teach."

Between exercising, he tells her that his dad has always wanted to pass the business down to him. There is nobody else to leave it to.

Zac asks her, as he does exercises, "what about you, any siblings or family in the area?"

She does not respond to the question, glancing at her watch, she tells him she has another patient to visit. Getting up, she grabs her bag, exercise bands, and tells him she will return on Friday. He gets on his crutches and walks with her to the door. As he closes the door, Maria calls from the other room.

"Zac, time for lunch."

When he sits down, he grimaces from leg pain. Maria looks at him and asks if he is content at the bay house with them. Zac drops the soft taco and says, "I wanted to talk to you and dad about living in the beach house. I am used to living alone, even though I will miss your cooking, Maria."

With that, the next day, Zac moved to the beach house. Maria agreed to bring food to him twice daily.

The weeks began to pass as Maria brought food to him two times a day and Mya visited for his therapy sessions three times, every week.

It is the first week of August now. One Friday, Mya arrived at the beach house to continue therapy. It is easier now. He performs the exercises with less effort as his leg heals. There is time during the sessions when Mya laughs at stories Zac shares from teaching. He tells Mya, "You know some people pay big money for punishment like this. You enjoy it. Are you a dominatrix in your free time?"

She leers at him before bursting out with laughter and telling him that she does not enjoy hurting people. "The progress of healing from the therapy I do, brings me joy. However, there will be pain along the way."

After saying that, she tells him that the session is over. She begins to gather her things to leave. Zac hands her the bands near him as she tries to pick them up. For a moment, they are holding hands. A brief pause occurs, as they look at one another before quickly looking away. An awkward silence follows before she stands and moves to the door, hurrying to leave.

She looks back at him before leaving through the door, "I will be back next week for the last few sessions."

He calls to her before she can get out the door, "I start driving next week. Let me take you out to dinner, for calling you a dominatrix."

She tells him that he does not need to drive so soon after wrecking his car. So, she offers to do the driving and he will pay for the dinner. He promises to take her to an upscale restaurant on the gulf.

That evening, he calls and
makes reservations at *The Crucible*. An
upscale restaurant near the beach. Zac
notifies Mya of the dinner plans and what
time to pick him up. When she tells her,
she says, "I have wanted to eat there for
some time now."

The next night, Mya arrives at
the beach house and discovers Zac is
waiting for her. He is wearing a black
dinner jacket, slacks, and starch white
shirt. She is wearing a cocktail dress,
bought earlier that day.

He looks at her when they get out, at the restaurant. "Wow, you look beautiful. Much better than the scrubs you normally wear."

She responds, "you look pretty good, too."

With a slight limp, he offers his arm to her. They walk together to the front entrance. An attendant opens the door and directs them inside. White tablecloths, candles, and formal attire filled the room. Immediately, Mya recognized local leaders, doctors, and a celebrity, in the room.

As they were being led to their table, Zac saw Chad and Piper. There was an exchange of glances but no greeting of any kind. Once seated, Zac ordered two glasses of wine and a basket of bread, until the entrees arrived.

They talked work and Zac made her laugh by telling her stories from teaching kids. They had a great evening together. The prime rib and lamb were wonderful. She had never been to such a place as the Crucible.

When dinner had finished and they drove back to the beach house, Mya walked Zac to the door, before driving back to her apartment. He leaned over to kiss on the cheek. She turned her head, to kiss him on the lips. Surprised, he pulled back after the kiss.

She wrapped her arms around his neck and pulled him closer. This time, the kiss was harder and more intentional. Zac had already unlocked his door before they kissed goodnight.

She took him by the hand and led him into the house, closing the door behind him. By the time they had reached the bedroom, they were both naked.

Sitting on the side of the bed, he pulls her near him. She is soft to the touch but firm, from the years of gymnastics and weight training. He is aroused by the nearness of her body to his. She smells of cocoa butter and reminds him of the beach during summer.

She nudges him back on the bed and climbs on top of him, pressing her inner thighs against his hips. As she kisses him, she moves slowly back and forth, rocking. The moans, at first soft, become louder. Moments later, the intensity of their hips moving against each other, cause their breathing to increase before the crescendo of pleasure brings the moment to a close.

Sweat droplets roll from Mya's head, dripping onto Zac's stomach, as she looks down at him. Still joined together, she collapses on him, kissing his neck before rolling over, settling next to him on the bed.

He says to her, "Mya, I am falling for you."

After a few moments, she tells him, "I like you too, but let us not get in a hurry. I am falling for you too. You make me feel special."

The next morning, Mya leaves before Zac can wake up and say goodbye. The sound of the door closing wakes him.

When he gets out of bed to make coffee, he sits in the living room, looking out at the beach. He thinks about Mya. He also begins to think about staying. He tells himself, "Maybe I will stay and run the company. I will give up my teaching job, for a chance with Mya."

Picking up his phone, he calls his school and takes a leave of absence. He will stay and run the company until his dad's health improves. It will give him a chance to pursue Mya. Now it is time to tell his dad and Maria.

He calls Maria and tells her that he will be at the bay house for supper. Maria is excited and begins to prepare a special meal after she hangs the phone up. When Tony picked him up, to drive him over to the house, Zac told him about his new plans.

"Hey dad, I have taken a leave from school. I am going to hang around and help you run things. It is important to me that you are strong enough. Next week, the doctor said I can start driving. I will meet with Chad next week. He has been running things alone for over 4 weeks. It is time to see those accounting ledgers."

Tony and Zac enter the house and his dad announced to Maria, the news of his staying.

"Maria, Zac is going to stay. He is not going back to school. He is going to run the office with Chad."

Zac assured his dad that the decision is not long term. He needed time to fully heal and to help with accounting in the office. The dinner was empanadas, mixed vegetables, and corn. The family was together around the same table and Zac was not fighting with his dad. It was a great evening.

The next morning Zac decided to get an early start on the accounting ledgers. He is not medically cleared to drive until Monday, but he felt great.

He calls Tony and asks where the ledgers are.

"Go to the office. Workers are putting furniture in the lobby. They are in Chad's safe. He will be there working."

Zac drives to the office. One car is in the lot. Going through the door, he takes the elevator up to the office level. He notices how clean everything appears. It has been years since he last walked through the offices. Cleaners usually do their job on Friday nights or weekends, preparing for the work week.

Stepping from the elevator, he walks down the red carpeted hall, leading to Chad's outer office. Opening the door, he hears sounds coming from the Chad's office. It sounds like Chad is moving furniture and rearranging. Concerned that he could hurt himself moving furniture, Zac rushes through the door, into the office.

"Hey!" Zac enters the room and stops. Chad has his back to the door, his pants around his ankles and is holding a girl's legs in the air. Chad looks over his shoulder at him.

Zac does not see who the girl is, until she sits up from the desk, she is lying on. It is Piper.

"Zac! What!"

He says nothing, turning around and leaving the room. He waits outside the door, in the foyer, digesting the scene he witnessed in the office.

Moments later, Piper exits the room, stopping only to curse at him for interrupting the intercourse she was having.

"You are a nuisance in my life, a virus."

Through the open door, Chad calls out to him, to come in the office. As soon as he enters the office, he apologizes to Chad for barging in on them.

"I am sorry, Chad. I did not mean to disturb whatever that was."

With a big smile he tells Zac, "We were celebrating. Piper is pregnant. She is going to marry me. We are planning to have the ceremony in Gulf Shores, her hometown."

Zac congratulates him and tells him that he hoped that they would be happy for many years.

"I do not expect an invitation but that is ok. I am happy for you, friend. She always wanted a family. You will make her happy."

Zac tells him about the review of the accounting ledgers. He explains the leave of absence from teaching to work within the company for a while. When Chad sits down to get the key to the safe, Zac sits in the brown leather chair facing him.

"Well Chad, what are your future plans, now that you will have a family?"

Chad reaches into the desk drawer, pulling out an envelope. He slides it across the desk to Zac. "This is my resignation. I know you are staying now. There is a company in Pensacola that offered me a partner position. Tony was not going to do that for me."

During the conversation, Chad thanks him for staying with the company. He talks about how kind Tony has been to him and how much he learned working at the company. "When you said that you and Piper would not be together, I made my move. I love her."

He also tells him how he began dating Piper after finding he and Piper would not get back together. Chad explains how he and Piper fell in love after a season of trips to the beach and spending weekends together.

Chad picks up a small box from the floor and begins walking out of the office. Before reaching the end of the carpeted hall, he tells Zac about the truck driver stealing lumber and selling it in the next town.

"I fired him yesterday. He was selling our lumber to construction companies one town over from us."

Zac watches the elevator doors close. Chad left with a small box of pictures and plaques from his desk. After 10 years, it all fit in a small box.

He sits in the high back leather chair behind the large oak desk. For the moment, he soaks up the idea of being president of the company, if he chooses to never teach again. If Mya were sharing the beach house with him, it would be far more enticing.

After he pulls the stack from the walk in safe, he sits them on the desk and turns on the lamp. He tells himself, "This will take some time."

The company office building is next to the bay. Several hours have now passed. The amber, pink, and oranges colors, accompanying a sunset, have crept into the office through the window facing the bay, where Zac works.

He thinks of Mya and her warm kisses and her embrace. The thought makes him close the ledger for another day. She is more important, he decides.

He drives with the window down, back to the house. As he drives, he watches the sun setting. When he reaches the house and goes inside, he hears Mya talking.

Pouring a cup of coffee, he walks out to the rear deck, overlooking at the beach. Sipping his coffee, he can hear Mya. "Oh no mom, I am so sorry. What do you want me to do? What happened? Ok, I will leave in the morning. How is Nikki?"

He watches as she ends the call. She walks out to stand next to him. She is crying. He puts his arms around her and asks what is wrong.

Mya looks at him, tears in her eyes, and tells him that her sister, Nikki, lost her husband this morning. He died suddenly. She tells him that she must go home to stand by her sister.

"Nikki lost her husband, after all."

Zac feels the need to stand by her during this time of loss and offers to go with her to pay respects. She looks at him and tells him, no.

"You cannot go to the funeral. I did not tell you about my sister or family for a reason. There are things that I am not ready to tell you about, right now."

The next morning, Zac cooks breakfast for Mya before she leaves. She tells him that she is going to be gone for a week. He kisses her before she leaves. She tells him to behave while she is gone.

A moving truck is next door. "New neighbors," he tells himself. A couple with three children. He waves at the couple and goes inside. After making toast and pouring a glass of juice, he sits on the deck and watches the beach fill with tourists.

That afternoon, there is a knock on his back door. It is the new neighbor. He opens the door.

"Hi, can I help you?" The man extends his hand.

"I am Gary. My family just moved in next door; it was my grandmother's. I saw your grill and wanted to borrow some charcoal, in exchange for a hamburger."

"I am Zac. Sure. Just take that bag on the storage bin."

Gary takes the bag, thanks Zac, and walks back over to his house. Soon, the smell of his grill draws him out the house.

"Zac, come on over and get a burger." Gary calls to him from his deck.

The day passed but he still missed Mya. The ten-hour drive to her hometown, gave her time to think. What will she say to her sister? They have talked little for the past 12 years, because of the fight.

Pulling in front of her childhood home, made her think of the day she left. Nikki is one year younger. Mya came home from college the first Christmas and discovered that Nikki had taken her boyfriend.

After driving from the university and arriving late one night, she tried not to wake her parents. When she opened the door, Nikki and Robert were having sex on the living room couch.

Robert was Mya's boyfriend before her sister slept with him. They had a fight and she got back in her car and drove to the next town. After staying in one of the hotels overnight, she returned to college.

One year later, Mya received word from her mom that Nikki and Robert were getting married. In fact, it was her mom who called her at the beach house and told her about the death.

She asked Mya to be with her sister during this time. Over the last few years, Mya has thought of calling Nikki. Their mom has been a moderator over the years, sharing events by talking to the girls individually.

Last year, Mya heard that Robert was battling cancer. He was exposed at the chemical plant, where he works. Nikki had a miscarriage about the same time, her second. These are the things her mother shares with her, since Nikki and Mya will not call one another.

Helen, Mya's mom, walks out to the car when Mya parks.

"Oh honey, I am so glad you are here. Things are a mess inside. Your sister needs you. Put the past behind you. She found out this morning that she is pregnant. Robert will never see his child."

Mya kisses her mom on the cheek and climbs the stairs, to the front door. When she walks into the room, Nikki is in a chair crying. Her auburn hair is not as bright, as in school. She looks up and sees Mya. She stands up, walks over to her, and wraps her arm around her sister's neck. Mya wraps her arms around her sister, and they hug for several minutes.

Suddenly, they both are crying.

"I should have called you a million times and talked," Mya told her.

"No, I should have apologized years ago. I wanted you in my life, no matter what.," Nikki responded.

Mya looks at her, as she wipes tears from her eyes, "I hear that I am going to be an aunt. I would love to be Aunt Mya. Sorry about Robert, Nikki."

Helen watches the girls talk. She begins to cry. Her children are finally mending their relationship. The women talk about babies, showers, and gifts before they realize there is a funeral to plan.

Nikki asked her father to make the arrangements. He missed Mya's arrival because he was meeting with the funeral director in town. Robert will be buried in the family plot, per Nikki's request.

Mya sends Zac a message before supper, that evening. *"Funeral tomorrow. Making the best of the trip. I will be back in two days."*

Nikki asks her if she is seeing anyone. Mya looks at her and pauses. Before she speaks, Nikki assures her that happiness and someone special in her life, is her greatest wish for her sister.

Mya tells her mom and Nikki about meeting Zac and falling for him. She describes the beach house and how happy she is. They congratulate her and tell her they want to meet him sometime.

Mya tells them, "November is three months away, but why don't all of you come down for Thanksgiving? We would love to have you."

The next day was the funeral. It was difficult to get through it. Nikki cried throughout the day. Mya cried with her through part of it. A death is a somber life event. There are those who are broken hearted and those who observe the broken hearted.

Mya made the trip to stand by Nikki. The sisters began to heal from their broken relationship. They stayed up late, laughing about childhood fun and decorations for the nursery.

Mya tells her, "I wish that we had made up, years ago. There were so many things I would have like to share with you." Nikki tells her that she feels lost without her husband.

The next morning, Mya plays the part of the grieving sister. Deep inside, she has a lot of animosity for the way Robert decided to cheat on her, with Nikki. The sadness she felt, was for Nikki. A widow walking behind the casket of her departed husband, is heart wrenching to watch. Caught in the emotions of comforting her sister, she cries with her.

The thing about a good cry, is that somehow you feel better. After the funeral, the family went back to Helen's house, to a table of food. In the south, people express their sympathy, with plates of food. In her hometown, which is commonplace. Platters of fried chicken, casseroles, and cakes of every kind, line the kitchen table. It looks more like a church homecoming than a funeral.

After staying with Helen and Nikki for five days, Mya decides that she is ready to get back to the Oceanside Panama City area. She spends her last night with her mom and sister playing Uno. They play until eventually everyone has fallen asleep in the floor.

The next morning, Nikki cooks omelets while Helen makes her homemade biscuits. Mya leaves Zac a voice mail. *Coming home soon. Expect me tomorrow afternoon. Love Mya.*

New Chapter

Zac drives to the Bay house to see his dad. For the last few days, while Mya is consoling her sister, he has been reviewing the accounting ledgers. There are a couple of errors. When Chad fired the truck driver, that resolved many of them.

At the Bay house, Zac finds luggage in his dad's office. Someone is going on a trip. While looking at the packed luggage, his dad enters the office.

"Hey dad, what is going on with luggage?"

Tony looks at him and asks him to sit down. "Maria and I are going to Costa Rica, to her hometown, for a while. Since you have taken a leave of absence, I am going with her. Her mom is sick. I am semi-retired now, you know."

Zac looks at his father, smiling from ear to ear. He has not seen him smile like that in a long time. He tells him, "Ok dad, but I need a way to contact you, if something happens." His dad agreed and promised to call or send word by the family attorney, Mason.

Tony left numbers for Maria, Mason, and himself. He told Zac, "I can be reached but please make sure it is an emergency. Mason has all the legal paperwork. You know if something happens to me or Maria."

While Zac and his dad are talking, Maria walks through the office, carrying a bag. She stops to kiss him on the head.

"We love you mijo." Zac smiles at his stepmother, in response to the kiss.

Zac tells his dad that he is going to ask Mya to move into the beach house. "I love her."

The next morning, Tony and Maria are taking a cab to the airport for an early flight to San Jose. So, Zac tells his parents goodbye and goes home. The next day, Mya scheduled to arrive in the afternoon, while he is at work.

The next day, Zac goes to work. When he gets home, at the end of the day, Mya will be waiting for him. He thinks about her while he is at work. It has been several days since she left. They have not spoken beyond a couple of text messages telling Zac that she is on her way back from her parent's house.

Without Chad or Tony in the office, meant that Zac was spread thin in terms of work that must be done. Yet, construction projects are on time. The beach condominium in Panama is going up, as well. He posted a job opening, that will take work off him. He has a replacement for Chad lined up. Things should improve soon.

Zac decides to leave the office early. He is ready to see Mya. He misses her. As he drives to the house, he thinks of everything he loves about her.

Mostly, he thinks of the things that arouse him like the curve of her hips, the smell of her skin, and the way she felt when her breasts pressed against him.

Turning into the driveway, he thought of their last night together. The image of her atop him, breasts bouncing, as she rode him. That moment flashed from his memory.

He has been anticipating the reunion, all day. When he walks through the door, he calls out her name. There is no response. Walking through the house, he can hear the shower running in the master bathroom.

He pushes the door open. Mya is standing in the shower, water and soap falling from body. The walls of glass around the shower, hide nothing from his gaze. When he clears his throat, she turns her head, pulls her hair back, and motions for him to join her.

Caught in the moment, Zac does not move at first. It did not take long for him to undress and step into the shower with her. Their time together in the shower was brief.

When they got out and had gotten dressed, Zac told her, "I have something for you." He reaches into his pocket and pulls out a key fob with one key on it.

"I want you to move in with me. This is your key to the house." She puts her arms around his neck and kisses him.

"Yes. I spend all my time here anyway."

Later that evening, he asks Mya about the trip and how her sister is doing. She tells him that Nikki is well, considering. Mya explains how she and her sister have been estranged because of Robert. She tells Zac that Nikki is pregnant and how sad she is that Robert will never see his child. Somehow it helped them to find peace between them.

"By the way, my family is coming for Thanksgiving."

Mya decorated the house for Halloween and welcomed children who were trick or treating the neighborhood. The two of them were building a home together. Mya was decorating the house and giving it new life. Zac was healing from the memories of his mom dying there.

Tony called to check in. "Hey son, how is the business? Tell me about the Panama condominiums." Tony told him about the coffee plantation and how happy he was. "I want you to find someone to stay in the bay house. Maria and I want someone to enjoy it. When we visit, we can stay somewhere else."

Thanksgiving was only three weeks away and there was so much to do. After hearing that Tony wanted to rent out the other house, Mya had the idea of letting the family stay there when they come for Thanksgiving.

The next day, she began to transform the house from Halloween décor to pumpkins, harvest wreaths, and fall decorations. She also began to use pumpkin spice scents and cinnamon. At one point, Zac told her to take a break. "All of the scents are giving me a headache."

A typical morning, now that they live together, meant breakfast and leaving home at the same time. There were some mornings when the kiss led to lovemaking, but they worked hard to safe it for the evenings. Suddenly, office work was more manageable Mya did not mind the last-minute therapy sessions, before going home.

One afternoon, when Mya had gotten home before him, Zac came in late. He walked through the door and immediately to the back of the house. Mya hears him call out, "hey, will you come to the bedroom for a minute?"

She was sitting on the sofa watching television. Thinking that they were going to have an afternoon encounter, she loosens her shirt and kicks her shoes off. When she walks into the bedroom, Zac is on his knees and holding out a ring box.

"Would you marry me and become Mrs. Meyers?"

Falling into his arms, she says yes and puts on the engagement ring. "I was expecting this at Christmas. I love you. I want to spend my life with you."

They talk about announcing it when the family comes for Thanksgiving dinner. There are so many things to do for the arrival. The bay house will be prepared as well. Tony and Maria have been gone for several weeks now. It needs to be cleaned before everyone gets in.

The next morning, Zac must be at the office early. He intends to take off the afternoon to clean the bay house before the arrival of family. Mya wakes up and feels sick. She eats breakfast, calls in that she will be late, then leaves for work an hour behind him.

While at work, she becomes sick again. Thinking it is a virus, she makes an appointment to see her doctor.

Meanwhile, the project manager has been doing well. Zac has only had to drive by worksites to see the progress made. When confronted with a large pay raise and good insurance, the general contractor, took the job offer. That hiring is the smartest decision Zac has made.

Zac leaves the office after lunch and goes directly to the bay house, to organize it. He could have hired someone easily but chose to do it himself, for his family and hers. Dusting, vacuuming, bed making, and stocking linen, was a labor of love.

He bought a wreath from a department store, on the way home, to go on the door. When he looked at the finished product, he felt satisfied, like most men would feel. After turning off lights and locking up, he went across the road to see if Mya was home from work. She told him she went in late, that morning.

When he arrived at the house and walked through the door, Mya was sitting on the back patio. It is November and the winds have begun to chill on the beach. She is wearing a sweatshirt. He walks out to stand with her, wrapping his arms around her waist and kissing her on the back of her neck.

"Hey, it is good to be home. It is getting cool out here, isn't it?" Mya looks over her shoulder and tells him that she was sick this morning.

He gently steps away, asking her if she has a virus. She says no. "I am pregnant. We are going to be parents." She was not sure how this would be received. Zac began shouting.

"I am going to be a dad. I cannot believe it."

"I want our family to be the first to know. Forgive me but I did not know how you would react to being a father so soon." All he could do is smile and hug her. He felt like everything was good in his life. He told her, "I am the luckiest man in the world. I have the most beautiful fiancé and she is having my baby. Perfect."

Two days later, Mya received a text message from Nikki. She and Helen are coming for holiday dinner.

Hey. Me and mom are coming for Thanksgiving. I cannot wait to see the beach and meet Zac.

Zac knew his dad and Maria would coming already. He left a message for him at the office.

"We are going to be back in town on Wednesday. We are flying on Wednesday and are scheduled to fly back Friday afternoon." Zac knew Tony enjoyed the coffee job because he wanted to get back to it."

Meanwhile, there were a lot of things to do for the dinner. Mya gave Zac a list and sent him to the grocery store to get ingredients for the feast. It had been a long time since he did the grocery store run for Thanksgiving.

In the days that passed, turkey was bought, and the stuffing recipe was confirmed. Before Helen departed home, she confirmed the recipe. She and Nikki were scheduled to arrive later in the day.

The anticipation of family coming in, the announcement of a baby, and the wedding to plan, gave them both nervous nauseas.

In less than 24 hours, the beach house would come alive with more activity than it has ever had. Both their families would arrive soon. They both have a sense of impending doom, like many who host family gatherings. Before going to bed, Tony sends Zac a message.

Chad sent a wedding invitation to me and Maria. Have a check sent to him by courier, a thousand dollars, from us both. He was helpful when I needed him. See you tomorrow.

The next morning, Mya heard from her mom.

Leaving home now. We should be there by the afternoon.

Zac follows Mya's orders and prepares the guest bedrooms for her sister and parents. They should arrive at any moment, now.

"Zac, go to the store and get some pie crusts. I am going to make some pumpkin pies." He leaves the beach house and drives to the local supermarket. A few minutes after he left, the doorbell rings.

When Mya opens the door, Helen and Nikki are standing with arms open. The women hug one another as Mya welcomes them to the house.

"I am so glad you came. Where is dad?" She notices the suitcases next to Nikki's car. Helen tells her that a situation happened at work and her dad could not come.

Mya tells them, "I will get Zac to bring your luggage in when he gets back from the supermarket."

Mya gives the women a tour of the house, going from room to room. She tells them about Tony, Maria, and Zac's mom. She explains that she died in the house and how attached Zac is to it.

When Zac returns from the market, he announces it. "Mya, I am back. Do you want me to get the luggage out there?" From the bedroom, he hears Mya yell, yes.

So, he brings the two pieces of luggage into the house. The women are now standing on the back patio, overlooking the beach. The sun will set soon. He can hear her telling Helen and Nikki about the spectacular sunsets and sunrises.

Mya hears Zac from inside the house. "Hey, where should I take this luggage?"

Mya tells Nikki, "C'mon and follow me. I want you to meet Zac." Standing at the edge of the living room, still holding the bags, he watches the women walk in from the patio.

He recognizes Mya's sister. It is… **Kimberly**. The women cross the kitchen and reach where he is standing. Mya looks at him. His heart rate has increased. His mind is racing, trying to figure out how to explain the acquaintance.

"Hey babe, this is Nikki. My only sister." Nikki locks eyes with him and shakes his hand.

Raising her eyebrows, she says, "hi I am Nikki. Nice to meet you. I would not have guessed you were sisters, no resemblance." Nikki tells him that she was adopted just before Mya was born.

Mya tells them to get more acquainted while she checked on Helen, who was now sitting in one of the patio chairs gazing at the setting sun.

She walks out to the back deck to sit with her mom. "Hey mom, it is a splendid view. Don't you agree?"

Helen looks back at her. "I can see why you love this place. It is breath taking."

Helen tells her, "Your dad and I are going to sell everything and move to a warmer climate. I have cousins in St. Augustine."

Mya sits at her mom's feet and holds her hand. She tells her how happy she is to have family at Thanksgiving. Especially this one because of the news she must share.

"Mom, Zac proposed to me. I said yes. We are going to have a baby. Nikki and I are going to make you a grand."

Helen smiled at Mya and a tear began to roll down her cheek. "I feel blessed to have my girls together again. Soon there will be grandchildren to love."

Inside, Nikki and Zac and talking. "I don't understand Kimberly." Zac tells her.

She tells him, "No, call me Nikki. That is what Mya has always called me. You need to forget about New Orleans. I will not lose my sister because of a man, again. Robert tore or relationship apart years ago. SAY NOTHING."

Zac looks back at her, noticing that Mya and Helen are   in from the patio. He looks at her and says, "Nikki, soon I will be your brother-in-law AND you will be our child's aunt. Mya is pregnant."

Nikki's eyes widened and her lips pursed before saying to him, in a hushed tone, "My sister's happiness is more important than New Orleans. I will not ruin our relationship again."

Helen walks up to Zac and kisses him on the cheek. "So, you are the young man who is joining our family."

Mya hushed her mom. Telling her, "I have not told Nikki. I wanted to share the good news with her while we were together."

Doing her best to look surprised, she hugs her sister and tells her, "I love you. Zac seems like a great guy."

Mya holds Nikki's hands and tells her that she is getting married and that she is pregnant.

"We are going to be pregnant at the same time, sis. Our children will grow up together just like we did."

Zac congratulates Nikki on her pregnancy. He tells her that it will be nice for the kids to grow up together.

Nikki tells him, "Just before Robert died, I found out that I was pregnant. He will never see his child after we suffered through two miscarriages."

A pause followed Nikki's statement before Mya reminded them all, "This is supposed to be a happy occasion. We have a meal to plan tomorrow."

During the evening, there were a few glances between Nikki and Zac. She would gently shake her head at him, mouth the word no and cover her lips with one finger.

Everyone stayed up, reminiscing about childhood memories, and laughing, until late into the evening. Nikki and Helen slept in the guest bedrooms upstairs. The beach house is large and has four bedrooms and three bathrooms. There is plenty of room for guests.

As Mya and Zac went to bed, he received a text message from Tony telling him they had arrived at the bay house and were going to bed.

Maria and I are in. We arrived at the bay house an hour ago.

His dad told him Maria was cooking a dish for the dinner, as well.

Mya, Helen, and Nikki got out of bed early and began cooking. When Zac got up, the house was full of activity and preparations for the afternoon feast. By the time Zac got out of the shower, the smell of pies and a turkey, filled the house.

The kitchen teamed with conversation and the accompanying sound pots and pans, as the women worked to make the dinner. By the time, Zac walked into the kitchen, Maria had joined the operation.

Feeling useless, Zac slipped out the front door and went across the street to talk to Tony. Instead of driving, he chose to walk the short distance and get some exercise. When he arrived, his dad was in the family room watching a game on the television.

"Hey, how are things on the plantation. I really thought you would be back to stay, by now."

Tony tells him about a man he met in San Juan, on the farm. He tells Zac about the process needed in farming coffee. "From our farm to your cup. I have learned it all."

His father tells him that he felt valuable on the farm. Nobody has ever wanted to listen to the old man. When the man is sick, Tony manages the workers and monitors the coffee farm procedures.

"Son, I love it here, but you do not need me. You already know how to run things. Tell me about Mya."

Zac tells Tony that they are going to be married. He also tells his dad that Mya is pregnant. Tony is happy but does not seem to be surprised.

"She is a sweet girl. I am proud to have her in the family." He then offers Zac a beer and invites him to watch the game with him.

"I will call Mason, the family attorney, after the wedding. Later, I will add the children." Zac glances at his dad, wondering why he used the plural.

"Surely you will have more than one. I would love to have a house full to spoil." Zac shook his head, not sure what to say.

"Hey, I got to get back across the street. I did not tell Mya where I went." And with that, he took his beer and walked back home.

Before he got out the door, his dad asked him if he sent the wedding gift to Chad and Piper. Zac yelled back through the house, yes.

The spread of food was so great that the leaves had to be added to the table for the meal and everyone to sit. Zac took pictures to commemorate the occasion.

Zac managed to get through dinner with minimal eye contact with Nikki. Helen talked about the wedding and the girl's forthcoming babies. It was truly a Thanksgiving.

At dinner, Tony announced that he and Maria were catching an early flight back because a tropical storm is expected to impact the coffee farm. Helen told Mya that they would leave early as well to get back.

"I want to get back home so Nikki does not miss work." Her expression changed when her mom mentioned work.

Mya looked at her and asked, "What is going on Nikki?" Her sister looked back at her and informed her that she took a leave of absence. In addition, that she cannot stay in Dillon with the memories of Robert around her.

"Mya, mom, and dad are moving to St. Augustine. I cannot live in Dillon alone." She remembered that Tony wanted the bay house rented out and offered the house to Nikki, while reading Zac's face for confirmation on the offer. He could only nod and confirm that it would be okay.

It happened fast. Someone who had a brief, yet intimate history with him, was going to live across the street. Suddenly, he felt anxiety all over his body.

He told himself, "This can go bad so many ways, for me."

Mya kissed her mom and sister goodbye. Zac reluctantly kissed Nikki on the cheek before getting a big hug and kiss from Helen.

"Boy, we are going to love you."

He thought to himself how true a statement that is, since he had already slept with two of the three women standing there.

Before the women made it out the door, Mya reminded them to come back for Christmas.

"We have a wedding to plan, and I need help to pull it off."

After the women had pulled out of the driveway, Zac thought he should call Tony. Then, he realized that they had left early and were on route to the coffee plantation in Costa Rica.

Sometime during the dinner, the women at the table decided to have the wedding during the Christmas holidays. Zac did not hear this since he had already sat down to watch the football game.

After Helen and Nikki left, Mya informed him of it. "We are going to have a small wedding when everyone comes back for the holiday. There will only be our family there. So, a lot less work to do.

There is a church with an outdoor courtyard and veranda, overlooking the water. With a wedding party of fifteen or less, including family, a couple of company executives, Chad, and Piper. Maya wanted to invite Piper. Afterall, she ran Zac into her arms, sort of.

After hearing Mya's plans, Zac goes down to the church and talks with the pastor. After a short conversation, the venue is available but will require time management. They will only have for two hours.

When he told Mya that he got the veranda, the next day, planning began. Nightly, the women talked for over a week until they felt that everything had been arranged.

After searching every dress and wedding shop, Mya found an ivory satin off the shoulder tea length dress, for the ceremony. When she sent a picture to Nikki for confirmation.

Nikki replied, "That is the one. Get it. The ivory dress against your tan, looks perfect."

She instructed Zac to leave it alone when she brought it home.

"It is bad luck for the groom to see the dress or the bride in the dress." She told him.

Zac had the restaurant where they had their first date, cater the small affair. He then found fairy lights, flowers, candles, and the other items on the list given to him, by Mya.

There will be no groomsmen or bridesmaids. The ceremony is scheduled for one hour before the sun sets.

Wedding Day

Finally, here, Zac waits in the front of the small gathering of family and friends. Candles surround the veranda. Gossamer is draped along the bannisters with lights wrapped within it. It is time for the ceremony to begin.

The multimedia director of the church, after the signaled is given, plays a soft symphonic version of the wedding march. Everyone stands as the double doors open.

David waits for Mya to step out onto the veranda and take his arm. Meanwhile, Zac waits patiently to see the woman he has chosen to spend his life with.

Mya emerges from the church, stepping out into view. She is wearing a white satin off the shoulder tea length dress. When looks to the front, the expression on Zac's face, was memorable.

When he saw Mya, he overwhelmed by her. Tears rolled down one of his cheeks. He smiled and mouthed the words "I love you," front the front of the room.

The women in attendance were moved by the gesture and tissues began to appear. Zac has waited what seems a lifetime to have someone as special as Mya.

Mya twenty weeks pregnant, was a glowing bride. Her father handed her off to Zac. After she wiped the tears from his cheek, she held his hand and kissed it.

The vows were traditional and took less time than the attendees expected. Afterwards, everyone walked out to the courtyard for the reception.

Chad and Piper missed the wedding but arrived for the reception. When they walked in, Chad pointed out who everyone was, to Piper. When she saw Nikki, she began to cross the courtyard. She intended to tell Mya that Zac had slept with her sister.

Piper had a lot of anger toward Zac, even though she is married happily to Chad. When she started the walk over to Mya, Chad went to the table of food.

All Piper could think of, was finding Zac in bed with Nikki. The trip to New Orleans was meant to be a makeup trip. They were going to get back together. No, she found her boyfriend naked in the bed with another woman.

Nikki sees Piper coming over and meets her in the courtyard with a clench and hug.

During the hug, she whispers into Piper's ear. "I will beat your ass in the middle of this courtyard and all these people, if you approach my sister, Mya. Tell your man, you are sick and want to leave. Do not make me talk to you again. You will not like it."

Nikki is a large woman compared the dainty Piper. She is almost six feet tall and has an 80-pound advantage on the former cheerleader. When Nikki whispers in her ear, Piper's eyes widened and her face portrayed fear.

After the clench, Nikki smiled and told Piper to feel better soon. The color had changed in her face. Nikki was determined to do anything to anyone, to keep her sister in her life.

It was not common for Nikki to get in fights. Helen and David used to joke that their daughter is more likely to be a bar bouncer than any other vocation.

When she let her go, Piper turned around and found Chad. Nikki watched the couple leave through the rear exit and walk to their car. When the car passed the wedding party before entering the road, she smiled at Piper and mouthed the words "I am watching you."

On the other side of the courtyard, Tony saw the women hug and Piper leave. When he approached Nikki for an explanation of what happened, she told him that Piper had gotten sick, and they had to leave.

Later, Chad sent them a message congratulating them and thanking them for the wedding gift.

The small cake and the few refreshments were eaten quickly. That was the intent. That way there are no leftovers.

Before everyone leaves, one of the women from the office, gets the wedding party together to take a picture. The fading sun casts amber and orange hues on the courtyard. Later, that picture will hang on the living room wall of the beach house.

The days following the wedding fly by. One afternoon, as the sisters sit on the back patio of the beach house, Nikki tells Mya, "I have taken leave from school. I am going to move down here. Can you find me a place to live?"

Mya first squeals in excitement. She is so excited to have her sister nearby. She then tells her that the bay house is available.

Mya's parents have already sold their home in Dillon and their belongings are on the way to the new house in St. Augustine, Florida.

When Mya calls Helen, she is told that the buyer wanted it as soon as possible.

"Honey, me, and your dad want warmer weather and more sunsets together. We want what you have."

When Mya gets off the phone, Nikki tells her, "I am not staying in Dillon by myself. The house reminds me of Robert. All the things I love have left. Me and the baby are coming down here."

It is Christmas Eve. The tree and many of the gifts, make it look like a baby shower. The area beneath the tree has diapers, baby seats, cribs to assemble, and several gifts wrapped.

The mood is one of love. The sisters are together and there is still hope for sister-in-law relationship between Zac and Nikki.

Meanwhile, Helen and David, drove to their new home after the Thanksgiving feast. Several days later, they are sitting on the rear porch of house on the beach, looking at the stars.

After forty years of marriage, they are spending this New Year's Eve in St. Augustine. They are many miles from the girl's childhood home. The new house looks out over the ocean. Holding hands and sitting in chairs, they watch the fireworks celebrating New Year.

The next day, Zac and Mya help Nikki move into the bay house. It is already furnished, so Nikki does not need anything other than her suitcase. She sold her home in Dillon with the furnishings. It is easier that way. This is a fresh start.

Zac promises to get her a temporary job until after the baby is born. He finds her a job at the office since she is organized. As a teacher, she was known to be better than most.

One month later, a gender reveal is organized. Zac arranges for a live feed, so David and Helen can watch from home. The reveal for the sisters is done by exchanging envelopes. They take turns opening the envelope of their sibling. Nikki will open Mya's and Mya will open Nikki's.

With the girl's parents watching from St. Augustine, they begin. Mya takes the envelope with Nikki's name on it. Opening it, she smiles as happy tears begin to pour.

"Nikki and Robert are having a little boy."

The grandparents celebrate from their home on the coast as they congratulate Nikki.

"I am going to call him Robby, after Robert."

Nikki then opens the envelope with Mya's name written on the outside. Nikki says nothing but begins to hug Mya. Looking at the screen she says, "Hey dad, you are going to have grandsons."

Zac and Mya kiss excitedly at the thought of a son. The couple had no gender preference. Nikki hugs Mya and Zac. He thinks for a moment about how awkward this feels. "I hope this gets easier in time."

Weeks pass, as the sisters' pregnancies end. Delivery day is coming. Mya is working more in the hospital than in-home therapy. Nikki answers the phone at the office and has streamlined the organization in Zac's department. Her ability to get people to do things, is amazing to him.

Nikki goes into labor while at the office. It is late April. Zac and Mya rush her to the hospital. In the delivery room, Mya coaches her sister through labor with breathing exercises and coercion to push. Helen and David could not come to the birthing. It is flu season, and they were exposed on bingo night.

When Mya went into labor, Nikki met them at the hospital. Zac stayed in the waiting room with Robby and Nikki coached Mya through labor and delivery. When Zac got to see Mya, she was beaming with pride. He looked at Nikki and thanked her for being with Mya through labor.

It is the beginning of the summer, and it has already been made memorable with the births of Robby and Kenny. The family had grown.

Zac had no siblings and other family, growing up. At least Kenny and Robby will have family to spend time together. Nourishing this bond, became a mission for him, telling himself, "Family never fades and lasts forever."

Soon, Nikki was teaching again, and Mya was working therapy cases. The company grew as construction projects increased. Zac hired a second project manager to monitor the increase in jobs.

The morning meeting that takes place in the boardroom, had to be moved to a larger space. The number of employees grew as the company thrived. The company has exceeded Tony and Zac's expectations.

Mason, the family lawyer, communicated with Zac's father on a weekly basis. So, Tony knew that the company was doing very well.

The first few years pass quickly. Summers slip by and the holidays come and go. Some days are spent at the beach house while others are spent on the back patio of the bay house, across the street.

One day, when everyone is together, Kenny runs to Nikki and says, "Aunt Nikki, Robby is sick and threw up on the floor."

She, along with Mya rush to find what happened. While Zac washes the deck, Nikki, and Mya check on the sick child. Robby has a fever and did not eat lunch, according to Nikki. After calling a friend, an appointment is made with a pediatrician.

That night, the parents take turns sitting with Robby, to monitor his fever and his pain. For the last couple of weeks, he has complained about his legs and feet hurting. It was dismissed a growing pain by the adults.

"Nikki, is there anything you want me to do? All of us are concerned about him, Kenny woke up and asked about Robby, as well."

Robby's eyes open and he looks up at his mom. "Why do my legs hurt?"

Nikki began to cry. As a mother, she is worried about her child. The house does not sleep much that night. Zac and Mya pace the floor. They are worried as well. Because of the time spent together every day, they share the concern with Nikki.

The next morning, Mya takes the day off go with Nikki and Robby to the doctor. Zac, worried about his nephew, keeps checking his phone throughout the morning. He is waiting patiently for an update on the diagnosis. He is concerned.

I take both women to hold Robby,
for the blood test. When it is finished, the
doctor prescribes medicine and tells them
to keep him indoor and out of the sun.

The night sweats and leg pains did
not stop. The fever came and went for the
next two days. When the doctor called, he
referred Robby to a specialist. All he said
was, "There are some things in his results
that require a specialist."

That afternoon, after driving to
Panama City, they arrive at the doctor's
office. The placard on the door said, *Dr.
Jaffe, Oncology.* Nikki and Mya suddenly
sense the magnitude of taking Robby to
this kind of doctor, cancer.

The appointment reveals that Robby seems to have a form of Leukemia. More blood tests are done to validate the diagnosis. The doctor believes that it will require chemotherapy and bone marrow from a donor.

Nikki and Mya break down and cry. If untreated, Robby could die. The doctor tells the women that it has been caught early and survival is extremely high. Treatment should be started as soon as possible after consulting with an orthopedic oncologist.

"I have confidence in the team that will work on your child's case. We will treat him and give him every chance possible to recover and live a normal life."

Following the biopsy of Robby's bone marrow, a chemotherapy medication was started. For one year, the family lived their lives around his illness. In time, his immune system was destroyed, to build back after the marrow transplant.

Members of the company, the hospital where Mya worked, and the family, were evaluated to be donors. A donor was found. That donor all the matching markers.

The following summer was spent going back and forth to the children's hospital nearby, getting lab tests. His body reacted positively to the treatments and the morrow transplant began to increase his cell counts.

When he saw the doctor, Nikki was reminded for him to avoid crowds, no uncooked food, keep his environment clean, and stay away from anyone sick. Afterall, his immune system is in restart mode.

Robby was weak after the procedure. Nikki and Mya took shifts looking after him at night. The first few were the scariest. One time, Nikki thought he had stopped breathing.

The beach house was converted into a small infirmary. It was sanitized and cleaned every day, sometimes two times. Helen and David were advised not to visit.

Christmas that year, was not normal. There were very few gifts, and the tree was not put up. Zac kept the television on a tree screensaver. The grandparents called for Christmas but did not come.

Robby was monitored by home health. Mya checked in on him during the day. Nikki video called him during the day, between classes at the school. The principal was empathetic after losing his son to illness two year previously.

This routine was conducted for one year. The following year, Robby had recovered. The boys started kindergarten together. Kenny gave Robby company at home during the recovery. They played when Robby was feeling up to it.

He recovered so well, that the doctor allowed him to play baseball when he reached middle school.

The boys spent every day together. One summer, they set up chairs and umbrellas on the beach, for money. At 16, Zac put them to work at the office. Robby had an interest in construction and asked questions when they spent time together.

As the boys grew, they show an interest in the family construction business. Zac never wanted to force it on them. They like it.

Kenny was good at math and spent time with the structural engineers. He learned how to read blueprints after working with the lead engineer and learning about load bearing.

As the years passed, Zac heard from Tony less and less. There were fewer phone calls and video calls. Eventually, they did not come home for holidays, they called and talked briefly.

Zac did not know that the family attorney, Mason, contacted Tony when Robby became sick. A call was made to Nikki, by Tony. He told her to stay in the house if she wanted.

It was a short call. He told her that she was considered family and she should not worry about anything. He would make sure that she had what she needed for Robby.

Soon afterwards, an envelope appeared on the kitchen counter at the bay house. Mason placed it there, for Nikki to find. In it, was a letter from Tony and a check for ten thousand dollars.

The letter stated that he looked at her as family and Robbie as his grandchild. He said, "Family sacrifices anything and everything to support its own." The money, he said, was so she could be with Robby as he recovered.

As time passed, Kenny and Robby grew and became more involved in the company's business. It takes many people to keep the company going.

Tony called the office switchboard one day, for Kenny. They talked briefly before Tony ended the conversation.

One week later, Mason called the family together at the house on the beach.

"I need everyone to come." He had a sallow expression. His eyes reflected a fatigue. "This morning, Maria called to say that Tony had died. She told me he died of cancer. It had been kept from everyone, at his request, until now."

A somber feeling filled the room. Kenny spoke. Saying, "I talked to granddad last week. He told me that he loved me. He apologized for not being here."

Kenny told them that he knew of the cancer and how he was not supposed to say anything. "Granddad knew he was dying and wished he could be here, with us. He said our family is the best thing he ever built. Protect this family. Defend it, no matter what."

When Nikki heard the message from him, she put a hand on Robby's arm and held Mya's hand. Zac had already put an arm around Kenny, who was next to him, and grabbed Mya's other hand.

Mason, before leaving, informed them of the reading of the will, on next day, in his office.

He said, "Everyone is expected to attend."

According to him, Tony had been cremated. Maria told him that it was his last request to be spread on their coffee plantation.

Zac did not know how to feel. He wanted to honor his father for not giving up on him. In the end, the best thing he could do, was bring Zac in and get out of the way.

The company is bigger than ever. Profits are soaring. They have offices in five cities along the Florida gulf coast. There are project managers in every one of those cities, overseeing the worksites.

Now, the morning meetings are done on video conference. It had to be done like this, because the staff did not have a room big enough to accommodate them. There are crews and managers working from Pensacola to Jacksonville.

The next morning, everyone met at Mason's office. Sitting around the room were Nikki, Robby, Kenny, Mya, and Zac. The boys are missing senior exams to attend the will reading.

Before beginning, he hands envelopes to everyone attending. Mya and Nikki receive two. Each of them, are sealed and addressed to them.

Mason begins, "I have been instructed to allow you a moment to review the contents of your envelope."

The sound of paper tearing fills the office, as each opens their designated envelope. Kenny and Robby erupt with excitement. Kenny says, "Granddad left us half of the company. We are millionaires Robby. How great. We will run it together one day."

Zac reads his letter. His expression is one of shock and disbelief. His letter was longer than the others. He asks Mason, "did you know about Nikki and dad talking and about Dr. Jaffe? Mya, I need to tell you something."

Mason interrupted Zac and told the boys, who had skipped exams for the reading, to go to school. After they had left, Zac continued.

"My dad told you I was at a workshop before coming home. Well, Nikki was there too. I met her there. She said her name was Kimberley."

Mya closed her letter, folding it, and placed it back in the envelope. She tells him that she already knew. Nikki had told her.

"One night, when Robby was recovering, she got drunk and told me that she had slept with you. She cried and begged me to forgive her. I did."

Mya told him how they made peace that night, drunk on the back deck of the beach house. She went on to say that he had treated Nikki and Robby like family. "I did not know about the surprise from Robby's procedure."

Nikki began to talk, "your dad called me while Robby was recovering. Dr. Jaffe is a friend of his, from school. In finding a donor, I also found out, you are Robby's dad. They are 99.97 percent positive. I have known for a while but said nothing. Tony made me promise. I told Mya when I got drunk."

Mason, after watching this, began the reading of the will.

I, *Anthony Myers, being of sound mind, do leave the following from my estate: to Nikki, I leave the bay house. This house is now a home for you and Robby. Mason will give you the deed. In addition, I leave you a monetary gift for the love you have brought to my family.*

To Mya: I leave the beach house. If anything, ever happens to Zac, it will be your piece of paradise. I am sure my son will take safe care of you and the grandchildren.

To Zac: I want my grandsons taken care of. I am leaving half of the company to you. The other half goes to my grandchildren, Kenny, and Robby.

Mason continued, "I have a letter to read, as well. It is from Mr. Meyers. It is his last thoughts for those here."

When Robby got sick, he was sent to Dr. Jacob Jaffe. He and I went to college together. There was a marrow match done. The donor who most closely matched him was Zac, his father. Jacob called to congratulate me. I found out that day.

My first concern was for Robby to be taken care of. My second concern was to let Nikki know that I will not allow her to destroy the family. I called her and we talked.

After that conversation, I determined that she is a perfect fit for the family. She gave me the indication that she would never hurt us.

Several years later now, I love her like a daughter. I gave her the bay house and cash for Robby's education. There is enough there to grow the coffee company, as well.

This family is stronger than ever. I have two grandsons and two daughters. Maria has chosen to stay in Costa Rica in the home we built here. The family and the company are safe in your hands, where I am leaving it.

Mya looks at Zac, "I have known for a long time. Nikki told me when she got drunk. For the past seventeen years, we have lived as a family. If my sister and I have made our peace, we will be ok. You raised Robby as your own. Well, he really is yours."

Nikki spoke, "I believe Robby will be ok. You have been the only father he has known."

She was right. In fact, Robby was mad at Nikki for not telling him sooner. Suddenly inheriting millions of dollars made him feel better.

The boys graduated high school and went to college together. Kenny earned a business degree while Robby got a structural engineering degree.

They are now the presidents of the company. Nikki quit teaching and works in the coffee import business. Zac and Mya help her part time when they are not traveling.

Legal papers, requiring signatures arrived the next week. There were provisions in the will for any children that followed. Nikki and Mya were given the coffee plantation.

They call the coffee company, *Two Sisters Coffee.* A couple of times a year, Mya, and Nikki, go to the plantation. Maria greets them at the farm. She does not drive much now, but still walks among the plants on the mountain side.

The first five years following Tony's death, Maria was flown in to spend the holiday with the family. The following year, Zac received a call from the new horticulturist for the farm. Maria was found dead on the mountainside, among the coffee plants.

When they found her, she was clutching a small picture in her hand. It was a picture of her and Tony after he had fallen on the hillside, years earlier. Zac knew in that moment, that her last thought was of Tony and their family. They were willing to do anything to find their one.

THE END

Made in the USA
Columbia, SC
27 November 2022